Whale Song Wedding

Coral Ripley

With special thanks to Sarah Hawkins
For James and Joshua Crouch

ORCHARD BOOKS

First published in Great Britain in 2021 by The Watts Publishing Group

1 3 5 7 9 10 8 6 4 2

A CIP catalogue record for this book
is available from the British Library.

ISBN 978 1 40836 378 2

Printed and bound in Great Britain by Clays Ltd, Elcograf S.p.A.

The paper and board used in this book are made from wood from responsible sources.

Orchard Books
An imprint of
Hachette Children's Group
Part of The Watts Publishing Group Limited
Carmelite House
50 Victoria Embankment
London EC4Y 0DZ

An Hachette UK Company
www.hachette.co.uk
www.hachettechildrens.co.uk

Contents

Chapter One

"There once was a mermaid with long golden hair . . ." The song rang out around the café. The Mermaid café was normally filled with happy chatter, but today all the customers were listening to the group of fishermen singing in the corner. "She had a tail as blue as the ocean deep . . ."

Emily crept round the tables, trying not

to make any noise as she put an omelette down in front of a lady, who smiled and nodded in thanks. She tiptoed back to the counter and turned to watch the singers too.

"And barnacles on her bum! Oh! Barnacles on her bum!" the fishermen bellowed. The accordion and guitar played a jaunty tune and everyone in the café laughed and cheered as the song finished and the fishermen bowed.

Emily's dad gave them a thumbs-up from the kitchen door. The Sunday Musical Brunch was his idea, and it was going well so far. Dad and Mum were a lot happier since they'd moved here and

opened The Mermaid Café, and so was
Emily. She loved living near the sea,
even if seagulls perched on her bedroom
windowsill and squawked noisily early
in the morning. Most of all, she loved
hanging out with her best friends, Grace
and Layla. But Emily's tummy turned
over as she thought about what was
going to happen next.

Grace went up to one of the fishermen,
her grandad, and took the guitar from
him. She sat down on a stool and started
tuning it, wearing a stripy top, jeans,
and a red headscarf over her blonde
hair. Layla was already on the makeshift
stage, tapping the microphone like a

professional musician and smoothing down the yellow skirt that matched the ribbons in her long, brown plaits. Emily's two friends were ready, the only thing missing . . . was her. She gulped as Layla waved her over.

Nervously, Emily took off her apron and went to stand next to her friends.

"Hi everyone, this is a song we wrote," Layla announced.

Grace gave Emily a supportive grin as she started playing. Together, they all started to sing:

"The oceans are big and beautiful,
The seas are wide and strong,
But we have to keep them clean,

And put right what we've got wrong.
Tell people to stop using plastic,
Say they can't dump it in the sea,
So that all the mermaids and fishes,
Can be safe and healthy and free."
Emily peeked out at the crowd.
Everyone was nodding and tapping their

feet. Over by the counter, Mum and Dad were recording the performance on their phones, looking proud as the girls reached the end of the song.

"We can all be Sea Keepers,
And work to save our seas.
So join us in our mission,
Save our oceans . . . please!"

Grace gave the guitar one last strum and Layla hit a high note. Everyone clapped. Emily felt relieved it was over! She hugged her best friends.

"That was brilliant!" Mum said, smiling as Emily went over to the counter.

"Blueberry pancakes and orange juice?" Dad asked. Emily nodded. Now that the

singing was over and her nerves had settled down, she was suddenly very hungry!

Dad piled pancakes on a plate, and Emily went to share them with her friends. Grace was sitting with her mum, grandad and little brother Henry. Her dog Barkley was lying under the table, happily eating a doggy treat. At the next table Layla was with her parents and her big sister Nadia. As Emily came over, Nadia went onstage and started singing a pop song.

"That was great. I want to be a Sea Keeper!" said Grace's brother.

Setting down the pancakes, Emily

glanced at her friends and they all shared a grin. No one else knew what it *really* meant to be a Sea Keeper!

Emily, Grace and Layla had been magically chosen to become Sea Keepers when they'd met a mermaid princess named Marina, and gone with her to the underwater city of Atlantis. There, the mermaids told them about the evil siren, Effluvia, who wanted to take over the mermaid kingdom. Effluvia was trying to steal the Golden Pearls that were filled with ancient mermaid magic. It was the Sea Keepers' job to find the Golden Pearls first and use their magic for good instead of evil.

Nadia finished her song, and everyone applauded. As she clapped, Emily saw something shimmer on her wrist – her bracelet was glowing. It was time for another Sea Keeper adventure! She quickly pulled her sleeve down over her bracelet. "Um, do you want to come up to my room?" she asked Grace and Layla. "I've got, er, something to show you upstairs?"

Grace nodded straight away, but Layla was still looking at the stage.

"Hang on, Mr Shah from school is about to sing," she said.

Emily elbowed her and showed her the bracelet. Layla gave an excited squeal as

she realised what was going on.

"We're just going upstairs for a few minutes," Grace told her family. She wasn't lying, because no time ever passed while they were off on an underwater adventure. So they could help the mermaids and still be back in time to listen to their teacher's song!

They rushed up the narrow stairs to Emily's bedroom in the flat above the café. Her big ginger cat, Nemo, was curled up on her bed as usual, and she could see the sea through her window. It looked so vast, it was hard to believe that in a few seconds they'd be out there somewhere, swimming with mermaids.

The girls said the words Marina had taught them:

"Take me to the ocean blue.
Sea Keepers to the rescue!"

In a flash of magic, they left Emily's room and found themselves underwater. Their legs had been turned into tails – they were mermaids again!

Chapter Two

Emily swished her gold tail and stared up at the beautiful palace made of shells in front of her.

"We've been here before!" Layla exclaimed.

Emily nodded. "It's Atlantis!" The palace was where the mermaid rulers, Queen Adrianna and King Caspian, lived with their son Prince Neptune

and daughter Princess Marina, who was swimming towards them now with an enormous grin on her face.

"Welcome back, Sea Keepers!" she said, sweeping Emily into a hug. Her pet dolphin, Kai, swam around them in delighted circles, clicking happily.

"I haven't seen you for *soooo* long!" Kai squealed.

Grace started playing with Kai the way she did with Barkley. The dolphin was as playful as an enormous underwater puppy!

"Have you changed your hair?" Layla asked. "It looks amazing!"

Marina grinned. Her hair was still a rainbow of pinks and purples, but it was plaited and pinned up around her purple shell crown, with only two long pink tendrils floating through the water. She patted her head. "Do you like it?"

"It's gorgeous!" Layla said. "Are you going somewhere fancy?"

"It's the reason I called you here," Marina said. "My cousin Meredith is getting married, and I wondered if you wanted to come to a mermaid wedding?"

"A mermaid wedding!" Layla gasped.

"So, hang on, we don't have to find a golden pearl?" Grace checked.

"And Effluvia hasn't caused any trouble?" Emily added.

"No pearl, no Effluvia – you're off duty today! This visit is just for fun!" Marina said with a laugh.

"Yippee!" Layla grabbed Marina's hands, spinning her round and round. Emily and Grace joined in too, laughing and squealing as they spun in the water.

"I think that's a yes!" Emily said to Marina. It was brilliant being in the mermaid world without needing to worry about evil Effluvia for once.

Marina led them inside. Emily looked around in wonder. The palace was just as grand as she remembered, and this time there were mermaids everywhere, chatting as they hung up beautiful garlands of seaweed and brightly coloured sea anemones. Excitement rippled through the water.

"Marina, there you are! Have you got the harp yet?" An older mermaid swam over, wringing her hands nervously. A fancy clamshell hat covered her blue

23

hair, and her tail was bright pink.

"Don't worry, Auntie Delphine, there's still plenty of time before the ceremony starts," Marina said. "Everyone, this is my auntie, Meredith's mother."

"Hello," Delphine said, nodding at them distractedly. "Marina, sweetie, I really think you should get the harp now. Without it, there can be no wedding."

"Fine, I'll go and get it," Marina reassured her aunt. She rolled her eyes as she led the girls down a corridor. "My auntie always fusses. But she's right – the harp is very important. It's filled with ancient magic from the Spirits of the Sea. It summons the whales, too, so that

24

they can sing at the ceremony. Because it's so precious, an old friend looks after it for us!"

The Sea Keepers followed Marina down the hallway to a huge mussel-shell door. Inside was a large clam, as big as a table, covered with barnacles. It was snoring gently.

Emily grinned as she saw the Mystic Clam. The old clam hadn't changed a bit since they'd last seen him!

"Oh, I feel so bad, but I have to wake him up!" Marina said, knocking gently on the clam's huge crinkled shell. The snoring stopped with a start and the shell slowly creaked open.

"Sea Keepers!" the old clam exclaimed. "You've come to visit me at long, long last . . ."

"Well, um . . ." Emily started.

The clam gave a rumbling laugh. "I'm joking! You're going to the wedding, of course."

"But we're very pleased to see you!" Layla said.

"And I you," the clam said fondly. "You'll be wanting the key, I suppose?"

He opened his shell wide to reveal a gold key resting inside. Marina took it out and swam over to unlock a chest at the other side of the room.

A moment later, she returned holding a

beautiful golden harp.

"Wonderful!" said the Mystic Clam as
Marina gave him back the key. "When
music and friendship work together, any
storm you can weather."

"What do you mean?" Emily asked curiously.

The old clam just gave a rumbling laugh instead of explaining. The girls were used to the way he spoke in riddles – they had to solve one every time they needed to find a Golden Pearl.

"What's so funny?" Layla asked him.

"Oh nothing," the Mystic Clam replied. "Now, if you'll excuse me, I need to take a nap. I am very, very old, you know."

As he started to snore again, they swam out of the room.

"It was nice to see the Mystic Clam again," Emily said.

"But what did he mean about music

28

and friendship?" Grace asked.

"I have no idea," Layla confessed.

"Ah Marina, you've got the harp!" Delphine said, beaming as they arrived back in the palace courtyard. "Can you give this to Meredith as well?" Delphine handed her a beautiful bouquet made from vibrant orange and pink anemones.

"Yes, Auntie." Marina shuffled the harp in her hands as she tried to take the bouquet.

"Here, let me help," said Layla. She took the harp from Marina, who smiled at her gratefully.

"Ugh, who invited the two-legs?" A surly-looking merman with green

29

hair and a shell necklace pushed past them, trailed by two friends.

"Neptune!" Marina turned to him crossly. "Be polite! The Sea Keepers have done so much for all of us in Atlantis!"

But the prince just sneered and swam on with his friends.

"I'm so sorry, ignore my rude brother," Marina said.

"It's OK, we know he's just angry that

he didn't get chosen to be Sea Keeper," Layla said.

"My brother is immature and rude too – but then he's only seven!" Grace added loudly.

The girls all giggled. Neptune must have heard because he swished his tail angrily, like Emily's cat Nemo did when he was about to pounce.

"Don't dawdle, Marina!" scolded Delphine. "You and Meredith were meant to have your scales shined half a tide ago!"

"Oops, sorry, Auntie," Marina said, laughing. "Why don't you girls come with me and help us get ready?"

31

"Ooh yes!" Layla agreed. "I loved getting ready when I was my cousin's bridesmaid. It'll be a girly pamper session – mermaid style!"

Marina led them into a grand bedroom. In the middle was a fancy four-poster bed with a huge scallopshell headboard and curtains made of bubbly white sea-foam. Sitting at a dressing table was a mermaid with a pearly white tail and long, curly brown hair. She was looking at her reflection in an oystershell mirror while a stripy blue angelfish fussed around her, trying to fix a seaweed veil on her head.

"Wow! You look radiant!" Marina squealed. "Girls, this is my cousin – the

bride. Meredith, meet Layla, Emily and Grace, the Sea Keepers!"

"I've heard so much about you!" Meredith said, turning to greet them.

Layla put the magic harp down on the bed and they all went to meet the bride. She looked radiant, with pearls glistening in her hair and her white scales shining like diamonds.

"There's no time for chit chat!" Delphine said, coming into the bedroom. She flapped her hands at Marina. "Sit down so we can get you ready!"

The princess sat down obediently and a suckerfish swam over and started cleaning her scales. "That really tickles!" Marina giggled, squirming.

The girls laughed too – but Meredith didn't even smile as another suckerfish swam around her fins.

34

"Are you OK?" Emily asked her.

"I'm so nervous!" Meredith said, holding her tummy.

Emily remembered how scared she'd been going up on stage to sing earlier. "Just take some deep breaths," she said reassuringly. "That really helps me when I'm feeling anxious."

Meredith breathed in and out and gave her a shaky smile.

The mermaids relaxed into being pampered, as preparations for the ceremony bustled around them. Two dolphins came in to discuss the wedding carriage. Delphine went out and came back with a plate of plankton

sandwiches, and offered them round.
Three mermaids came in with garlands
of anemones. A cloud of zebrafish
brought an ice sculpture from the Arctic

mermaids, an eel delivered a card
for the bride and a turtle presented a
coral bracelet – a gift from the tropical
mermaids.

"Are all weddings this exciting?" Emily
asked, nibbling on a sandwich. "I've
never been to a human wedding – let
alone a mermaid one."

Layla nodded. "My cousin's wedding
went on for three days! It was so much
fun. There was lots of delicious food
and the dancing lasted all night long.
I wonder if there's dancing at mermaid
weddings?"

"Well, there's definitely going to be
music." Grace glanced over at the bed,

then looked confused. "Wait – where's the harp?" she asked.

Marina looked around and gasped. There was nothing on the bed. The magic harp was gone!

Chapter Three

"Guards!" Delphine shrieked, and soon the room was even busier with the palace guards searching for the magic harp. They looked in every corner, but it was nowhere to be found.

"My wedding is ruined!" Meredith sobbed.

"I'm sure the whales can sing without it," Emily tried to reassure her.

Marina shook her head. "You don't understand, the harp's magic is essential to a mermaid wedding. Without it, they can't get married!"

"Don't worry, we'll find it," Grace said.

"And your wedding will be perfect!" Layla told Meredith.

"Can we use some mermaid magic to track it down?" Emily asked.

"Maybe . . ." Marina said.

As she was thinking, King Caspian and Queen Adrianna swept into the room, followed by Prince Neptune, who was looking very smug.

"I can't believe you lost the harp, Marina!" Adrianna said sternly. "It only

leaves the Mystic Clam's protection just before a wedding. How could you be so careless?"

"I'm sorry!" Marina said. "I don't know how it could have happened. We never left it unattended. Maybe we can use our magic to find out where it is?"

"Then we'll go and get it back," Emily promised.

Adrianna gave a sharp nod, then she opened her arms wide and began to sing, her beautiful voice echoing around the bedroom.

"Mermaid magic let me see,
Where the ancient harp could be."

A shimmering bubble the size of a

beachball appeared in front of her. Everyone peered into it. Inside the bubble was a picture of a sandy beach with waves lapping at the shore. There was a harbour with boats bobbing on it, and a town full of colourful painted houses. And there, on the sand, was the magic harp!

Emily gasped. She knew that place!

Grace and Layla recognised it too.

"It's Sandcombe!" Grace said. "That's where we live. But what's the harp doing there?"

"And what's that under the water?" Emily asked, frowning. In the harbour, dark shapes lurked just below the surface.

"It's the humpback choir. They
must have followed the harp," Marina
whispered in dismay.

The silence was broken by a slow clap.
Neptune swam forward. "Very nice

acting, Sea Keepers, I almost believe you!"

"What do you mean?" Grace replied.

"YOU stole the harp!" Neptune accused them. "It was safe for hundreds of years until you arrived, and now suddenly it's gone! We never should have trusted some two-legs to be our Sea Keepers. All humans do is hurt sea creatures and steal our magic."

Emily gasped.

"We would never do that!" Layla declared.

"You were the ones who had the harp last, and now it's in the place where you live," Neptune said angrily. "And what's

44

that?" He pointed at the harp. There was something yellow tangled in the strings – one of Layla's hair ribbons.

Layla touched her other ribbon. "That must have happened when I was carrying it," she explained. "I promise we didn't steal it!"

But the angelfish were whispering, and Meredith was watching the girls with a disappointed look on her face.

Delphine put her arm around Meredith. "Neptune's right," she said. "We never should have trusted humans. I'm sorry but it's true."

"They should be banished like the sirens were," Prince Neptune said.

"Wait!" Marina swam out in front of the Sea Keepers. "Grace, Emily and Layla have helped us so much! They didn't even know about the harp! And they were with me the whole time. They couldn't have taken the harp – and besides, they wouldn't."

"Of course we wouldn't!" Layla said indignantly.

Neptune shrugged. "I don't believe a word they say. They probably got someone else to steal it for them. Why else would it be on dry land?"

"It wasn't us!" Grace said crossly.

"We'll prove it. Let us go and get the harp back," Emily said.

Queen Adrianna looked from Neptune to Marina, then nodded at the girls. "You may have a chance to prove your innocence," she said. "But if this is a trick and you fail to return  the harp, you will be banished for good. Marina, you are not to use your magic to help them. Understood?"

Marina nodded. "Yes, Mother."

"We'll get the harp," Emily said firmly.

"And save your wedding," Layla promised Meredith.

"Then *you'll* have to apologise!" Grace told Neptune. He tossed his head and gave a snort.

"Please hurry," Meredith told them as Marina led them out of the room.

"I can't believe they think we'd do that!" Layla said as they headed out of the palace. Mermaids fell silent as they swam past, and the fish looked at them suspiciously.

"We have to get to Sandcombe, fast," Emily said.

"I've got an idea," Marina told them.

"Your mum said you can't use your

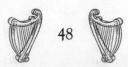

48

magic," Layla reminded her.

"I don't need to!" Marina said mischievously. She took them through gardens with coral sculptures and beautiful seaweeds, past a rock maze and up to some stables. "The royal dolphins will get us there much faster," Marina said.

"Did you say 'us'?" Emily asked.

"I'm coming with you. I know you didn't take the harp, and I'm going to help you prove it!" Marina said. "There's nothing my parents can do about it!"

She opened the stable doors. It was just like a horse stable, except peeking over the stall doors were dolphins!

They clicked happily as the princess went over and stroked their sleek, silver noses. "Meet Bolt and Dash," she said, opening the doors to their stalls. She started looping reins around the dolphins' noses, then attached them to a carriage in the corner.

"This is Neptune's racing carriage," she said with a mischievous grin. "It's the fastest one we have. I'm sure my dear brother would be glad to lend it to us."

"Won't you get in trouble?" Layla asked.

"I'm sure they'll forgive me when we return with the harp," Marina said with a shrug.

"I wonder who took it," said Emily.

"I've been thinking about that," Grace said, swimming up and sitting inside the carriage. "So many creatures came into the room. There were the zebrafish and two dolphins and the mermaids with the garland."

51

"Don't forget the turtle, and the eel," Emily added as she got in.

"Well, whoever took it is bound to be at Sandcombe!" Marina said, sitting at the front of the carriage and grasping the reins. "Hold on tight!" She clicked her tongue and the dolphins shot off. "Let's go track down the thief!"

Chapter Four

The dolphins sped through the water, pulling the racing carriage behind them. Emily, Grace, Layla and Marina clung on tight. It was like being on the world's fastest water ride!

"Neptune might be a pain, but he's good at picking racing carriages!" Grace said as they finally slowed down.

"Sandcombe is just ahead of us,"

Marina said, pointing.

"What's that noise?" Grace asked as a ghostly noise echoed through the water.

"It sounds a bit like an owl hooting,'" Layla said.

"I'm sure I've heard it before," Emily said. Maybe it had been in one of the animal programmes she and her parents

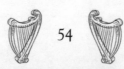

loved watching on television. It was a
high and eerie noise, but beautiful too.

"It's the whales!" Marina said.

Up ahead they could see six huge, dark
shapes in the water. They were calling in
ooooohs and rumbles and high-pitched
squeals that reverberated through the
water around them.

"Oh wow!" Emily whispered. She'd met lots of different sea creatures, but meeting a new one never stopped being amazing.

Marina pulled the dolphin carriage up next to the pod, and they watched in wonder as the enormous whales swam in a slow loop, heading to the surface to breathe and then diving down again.

"I've never seen whales in Sandcombe harbour before," Grace said.

"They shouldn't be here, the water is very shallow," Marina said anxiously. "It must be because they followed the harp."

"Right, let's grab it and get back to the palace!" Grace said. "I'll go and look for it." She shot out of the carriage

and headed to the
surface. When she
returned a second
later, her face was
serious. "The harp's
not on the shore any
more!" she said.

The others swam
out of the carriage.
Marina went over
to the dolphins.
"Thank you, my
friends," she said,
stroking their noses.
"You'd better go
back to the palace

before Neptune misses you. We might be a while."

"Thank you!" the girls called.

"Good luck!" Dash said as the dolphins raced back home.

"The tide is going out," Marina said. "We have to get the whales to go to deeper water. If they stay here, they'll get stranded!"

"Let's talk to them," Layla said. "Maybe if we explain, we can get them to move."

They swam up to the whales. They were even bigger up close – each one was larger than a bus and even the baby one was the size of a car! Emily gasped as one

swam right next to her. Its tummy and the sides of its fins were white, and its throat was covered with long stripes and scarred with scratches and circles. There were knobbly bits on its head, and as it passed she could see clumps of barnacles attached to its fins and tail.

Marina swam up to the biggest whale, who had a crown of white barnacles on her head. The whale's tiny eyes blinked at them.

Marina bowed. "Great whale, it is a pleasure to meet you and your pod. I am Princess Marina and these are the Sea Keepers: Layla, Grace and Emily."

"Hellloooooooo, I am Viooooooola," the

whale said in a deep, sing-songy voice. "Can you tell us where the wedding is, please?"

"Meredith's wedding?" Grace asked.

"Yes," Viola said. "We folloooooowed the harp."

"The harp's been stolen!" Emily explained.

"Stooooolen?" said the whale, confused.

"We'll explain later," said Grace. "Please, you need to get into deeper water—"

"Oh, you're in deep water, all right," came a voice from behind them. "Isn't that what you two-legs say when you're in trouble? Because you're in serious

trouble right now!"

The girls turned to see a mermaid with midnight blue hair and a purple tail. Next to her bobbed an anglerfish with a light hanging over his sharp, protruding teeth. The mermaid was stroking an eel who was wrapped around her shoulders like a scarf – and she was holding the magic harp!

"Effluvia!" Marina gasped. "What are you doing here?"

"You've made a mistake," Grace told the siren. "We're not here to look for a Golden Pearl."

"We were just at the palace for the wedding," Emily tried to explain.

"Yeah, so you really don't need to stay here!" Layla added.

"Why would I go, when I've gone to so much trouble to get this harp?" Effluvia said sweetly. The siren's voice was always so beautiful, but Emily knew it was powerful, too. Her song was so captivating that it could enchant you and make you do whatever she wanted.

Sure enough, the eel curved around her neck had the glowing yellow eyes that showed it was under her spell.

"That eel came into the dressing room!" Emily said, suddenly realising what had happened. "That's how you stole the harp!"

"Oh yes, Gulper here is quite talented!" Effluvia purred. "Why don't you show them what you can do, my slippery friend?"

Gulper gave an evil grin and slid off Effluvia's shoulders. Then he opened his mouth – wider and wider and wider. His jaws were absolutely huge!

"It was all too easy for him to sneak

in and gulp down the harp," Effluvia
gloated. "Look!" Before anyone could
react, she picked up the anglerfish and
dropped him into Gulper's open jaws.
The eel snapped his jaws shut and
swallowed the fish whole!

Layla, Emily, Grace and Marina were
horrified. They didn't like Effluvia's
sidekick, Fang, but he didn't deserve to
be eaten!

"Let him out!" Grace demanded.

A muffled noise came from Gulper's
throat, and the girls could see
the faint glow from Fang's light.
"Effffffuufuummpft! Lfft mfftt oouufft!"
he called from inside the eel.

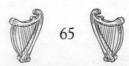

65

Effluvia rolled her eyes, then waved at Gulper. "Spit him out," she drawled as if she was bored.

Gulper opened his mouth and coughed Fang up. The anglerfish darted over to Effluvia and hung on to her tail, shivering. "Oh, thank you, Effluvia, you are so kind, so merciful—"

"Silence!" Effluvia waved her hand across the harp, and a delicate sound filled the water as the harp began to play a beautiful melody. The whales reacted, turning to the harp and singing the same notes back.

"If you don't want a Golden Pearl, what *do* you want?" Layla asked.

66

Effluvia strummed the harp again. "I want to get you Sea Keepers banished. And I'd say that plan is going pretty well so far. Without you to stop me, and a harp full of ancient magic by my side" –

she strummed the harp again and gave
a horrible smile – "there will be nobody
to stop me from releasing my siren sisters
and ruling Atlantis for ever!"

Chapter Five

Effluvia swam closer to the shore, her laughter chiming with the harp and the whale song. The water was so shallow that her tail kicked up clouds of sand from the seabed. She strummed the harp as she went and the whales all followed the beautiful melody, singing in reply as they swam after her.

"She's trying to get them beached!"

Marina exclaimed. She kicked her flippers and chased after Viola. "Stop! Don't let the pod follow her. It's a trap!"

Luckily, Viola stopped. "Dooooon't folloooow the harp," the great whale commanded in her sing-song voice.

All the whales obeyed. Layla, Emily and Grace breathed a sigh of relief.

Effluvia kept playing the harp, the intoxicating music floating through the water. The whales sang along, but no one moved – except the small calf, who slipped out from under his mother's fin and sped towards the irresistible sound of the music.

"Piper!" his mother cried out in

warning. But the baby whale had gone too far and the water was too shallow for him to turn around.

"Help!" he called as his tummy dragged on the seabed. It was no good, he was stuck! He lay on the beach, the water lapping around him as the waves went in and out.

"Piper!" his mother shouted again as the baby squealed miserably. She started to swim towards him.

"No, wait! Don't go after him, you'll just get stuck too!" shouted Layla, as Grace waved her arms in warning.

Emily raced up to the mother whale's fin and pulled on it with all her strength,

trying to stop her. But the huge creature didn't even notice.

"Cadence!" Viola moved in front of her, and the rest of the pod followed, forming a wall between Cadence and the shallow water.

"Nooooo!" Cadence sobbed, cries wracking her body. "Let me get past! That's my baby!"

Layla swam up to Cadence's head and looked her in the eye. "We'll help Piper, I promise," she said. "But you can't go any further or you'll get beached too."

Cadence kept sobbing, but she stopped trying to swim into the shallow water.

"Pity," Effluvia snapped as she swam

73

around the wall of whales. "But still, one beached whale is enough to destroy the whole pod. They won't leave without the baby, and when the tide goes out they'll all be stuck!" She strummed on the harp and smirked. "That should give me enough time to figure out how to use this thing's powers. Come, Gulper," she gloated. "Let's go get you a snack."

Laughing gleefully, Effluvia swam away from the harbour, taking the harp with her.

"I'd like a snack, Effluvia. Can I have one too?" Fang whined as he trailed after her.

Emily felt like crying as she thought

about the whales being stuck in Sandcombe harbour at low tide. When the tide went out, the harbour was just thick mud. She and Layla and Grace had spent many happy hours there looking at the crabs and other creatures that lived in the rock pools. Mum had even collected seaweed to cook once, although it had tasted even worse than the mermaids' plankton sandwiches. Emily imagined the whole whale pod lying helpless on the mud and shook her head fiercely. She wouldn't let Piper still be there when the tide went out!

"Marina, can you please make us human again? Then we can get him

back into the water!" she said. She knew Marina wasn't supposed to be using her magic, but this was an emergency.

"Yes!" Layla said.

"We can't do anything from here," Grace agreed.

Marina nodded, then started to sing in her beautiful voice:

"Send the Sea Keepers back to land,
We need human help to lend a hand."

The mermaid magic swirled around them and the girls swam up to the surface. As her face hit the fresh air, Emily tried to kick her tail and realised it wasn't there. Her legs were back, and her jeans were sopping wet!

"We should have got out of the water first, I'm soaking!" Layla groaned as they stumbled on to the wet sand next to the baby whale.

"Help me . . ." moaned Piper.

"Don't worry, we're going to get you out of here," Emily promised, stroking his smooth side.

Piper gave another low moan, then a whistle.

Emily looked out to sea. The rest of the pod shouted encouragement to Piper from the harbour as they took it in turns to come to the surface to breathe. Near them she spotted Marina's pinky-purple hair as the mermaid bobbed in the water, watching them.

"I want my mummy!'" Piper wailed.

Emily stroked his side again, feeling so sorry for the baby whale.

"We'll have you back in the water in no time!" Layla said cheerfully.

Grace didn't look so sure. "He's so much bigger than he looked underwater,"

she muttered. "I'm not sure we're going to be able to move him."

"If we can just get him unstuck . . ." said Emily. She started digging at the sand by Piper's tail.

Grace and Layla began to dig, too. Piper sighed and huffed water from his blowhole, raining water down on them. "Hey! I'm wet enough already," Layla joked, trying to make the baby whale laugh.

Piper tried to turn to look at them, and his huge tail almost knocked Grace off her feet.

"Whoa!" she yelled out.

"Sorry!" said Piper.

"Try to stay calm," said Emily soothingly. She stroked the baby whale and he quietened down, his body staying still apart from the occasional sob.

The girls dug out more sand, then they tried to push him again. Emily leaned her whole body against Piper's tail, but

it still wouldn't budge.

Marina swam over and sat in the shallows, keeping her tail hidden underwater. There wasn't anyone around, but she had to be careful no one spotted her – humans weren't supposed to know that mermaids existed!

"How's it going?" she asked the girls.

"It's no good!" Grace said. "We need more help!"

They looked around, but there was no one in sight.

"I can make myself human," Marina suggested.

"You can do that?" Layla asked.

"I'm not meant to." Marina looked pale but determined. "It's against the mermaid code – I could be banished if anyone finds out."

"Banished from Atlantis?" Layla asked.

Marina shook her head. "From being a mermaid."

Emily gasped. She loved being a

mermaid – but she loved going home again afterwards. She wouldn't want to be stuck as a mermaid for ever. If Marina became human, she might never be able to go home or see her friends and family again!

"We can't let you do that," Layla said.

"It's much too risky," agreed Emily.

"We can get someone else to help," Grace said, looking around again. On sunny days, the harbour was usually busy with families making sandcastles, fishermen hauling in their catch, and people walking their dogs and eating ice creams by the sea. But today, because the skies were grey, it was empty.

Piper gave a high-pitched moan that shook his whole body.

"It's OK." Emily patted his side.

But as he cried out there was a huge splash and a flurry of activity from the pod.

"Cadence is trying to get past the other whales again!" Marina said. "There's no time to get anyone else! I've got to help."

Before the girls could say anything, Marina opened her mouth and started to sing:

"I am needed to lend a hand.
Let me walk upon the land!"

Mermaid magic bubbled in the shallow water, and suddenly Marina's sparkling

turquoise tail was replaced with a blue wetsuit ending in two long legs and bare feet with toenails painted the same purple as her flippers.

Marina was human!

Chapter Six

Marina stumbled out of the water and on to the sandy beach.

"Are legs always so . . . wobbly?" the mermaid gasped. She took a few more steps then tripped and landed on her bottom.

"Whoops!" giggled Grace, running over to help her.

Marina stared at her toes in amazement

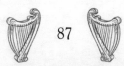

as she wriggled them.

"It's strange at first, but you'll get used to it," Layla told her.

"Um, we don't have much time," Emily said, looking at where the whales were still churning up the water.

"Help me up!" Marina said.

The girls pulled her to her feet, and

together they staggered over to where
the baby whale was lying on the beach.

Piper waved his flippers and his tail as
they approached.

"Try and keep still," Emily told him.
This time, Piper didn't stop flailing. The
baby whale let out a loud moan. Out in
the harbour, his mum thrashed her tail
and swam towards him.

"Cadence, don't come any nearer!"
Grace called in warning.

But the whale didn't seem to be
listening either. She swam even closer to
the beach.

"Maybe she'll listen to Viola," said
Layla, pointing to a head with barnacles

on it, rising out of the water.

"Viola!" called Marina. "Tell Cadence
not to come any closer."

The pod leader's only reply was a spurt
of water from her blowhole.

"Why aren't they listening?" asked
Marina in frustration.

Just then, Emily realised something. It
wasn't that the whales weren't listening
– they couldn't understand them!
Their mermaid powers weren't working
anymore, now that Marina was human.

"We have to get Piper back in the
water," Emily said urgently.

"OK, on the count of three – one, two,
three . . . PUSH!" Grace instructed. They

90

all heaved as hard as they could. Piper moved – but only a tiny bit.

They tried again, pushing with all their might against the whale's side, but it was like trying to move a house. Even with four of them leaning on Piper, he didn't get any closer to the waves.

"We're just not strong enough," Layla said, sighing.

"It was worth a try," said Marina. "I'd better change back before anyone notices I broke the rules." She stepped into the water and sang a magic song:

"Mermaid magic, come to me.
Take me back beneath the sea."

The girls waited for the magical

bubbles to surround her, but nothing
happened.

Marina went pale. She tried singing the
magic words once more. Again, nothing
happened.

"I think . . . I've
been banished,"
she said,
bursting
into tears.
"But how
did anyone
find out?
I was only
human for a few
minutes, and it

was only to help the whales—"

Emily ran to give her a hug. A terrible thought occurred to her – had Marina given up being a mermaid princess for nothing?

"It's not over," Grace said firmly. "First we're going to get Piper back in the water, and then we'll find a way to get you home."

Marina nodded bravely.

Piper gave another sad moan.

Emily put her hand on his side to try and reassure him and noticed that the whale's skin was dry. "We need to keep him wet!" she said.

Layla found an abandoned bucket, and

Grace found an old coffee cup that had been washed ashore. For once the rubbish people left in the sea was useful. They started pouring water over Piper's sides, and he wriggled gratefully.

"We need to get help," Layla said.

"OK," Grace organised them. "Emily, why don't you go to the Mermaid Café and get everyone? The rest of us will stay here and keep Piper wet."

"Great idea!" Emily said. Leaving Marina, Layla and Grace pouring water on Piper, she hurried over the sand and up the steps on to the cobblestone street.

Emily raced up the hill as fast as she could, panting for breath as she ran.

Eventually she saw the familiar sign with the kind-looking mermaid on it, and the swirly writing spelling out The Mermaid Café. Through the window, she could see everyone at the tables, watching the teacher singing on the stage.

For a second, Emily paused, wishing Layla had come instead. Her friend would know exactly how to get everyone's attention. This was going to be even more embarrassing than singing onstage! Then Emily thought about Piper down on the beach, and Cadence and the rest of the whales in the water, desperate to get to him. Effluvia was right – if they didn't save Piper the whole

pod would get beached. They might even die. Taking a deep breath, she flung open the door, making the bell jingle wildly.

"There's a whale stranded in the harbour!" she yelled.

Mr Shah stopped performing, and everyone in the café started talking at once.

Layla's grandad stood and beckoned for everyone to follow him. "Let's go down to the beach – we'll need all the help we can get."

The customers hurried out of the café, the bell jingling again and again as they went through the door.

Emily's parents pulled off their aprons and came over, looking puzzled. "I thought you girls were upstairs! How did you know it was there?" Mum asked.

"Oh, we saw something from my bedroom window and went out the back way to look," Emily stuttered. She felt awful lying to her parents, but she couldn't tell them the truth about being a Sea Keeper! "Grace and Layla are still on the beach. We have to hurry!"

Mum and Dad locked the café door and they rushed down to the seafront. It was much easier going down the hill to the beach than it was going up it.

Mum gasped as she saw Piper lying groaning on the sand. "Oh the poor thing," she said.

"It's only a young whale," Emily said.

"Look, there's the rest of the pod!" Dad

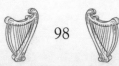

pointed at the whales in the harbour. Emily breathed a sigh of relief – Cadence hadn't beached herself, yet. But the tide had gone out even further in the brief time she'd been away.

She went over to where Grace, Layla and Marina were sitting next to Piper's head, trying to comfort him.

Layla's grandad was striding around, talking on his phone. "The whale rescue expert says we shouldn't try and move it," he told them when he had finished the call. "They'll get here as soon as they can, but in the meantime we should wet sheets and put them over the whale to keep it from drying out."

"Maybe we could use tablecloths from the café instead of sheets!" Emily suggested.

"Yes, I'll get them." Mum headed back up to the café.

"Everything OK?" Emily whispered to the others.

"Cadence keeps trying to come up, but the others are stopping her," Layla told her.

"It's so hard not being able to talk to them!" Marina said sadly.

"The whale experts will know what to do," Grace said.

"I just hope— *EEEEK!* What is THAT?" Marina broke off mid-sentence

as a brown blur raced up to them,
barking excitedly as he leapt up at Grace
and licked her on the face.

"Down, Barkely!" Grace caught hold of

his collar, laughing in surprise. "This is my dog, Barkley."

Marina scrambled backwards across the sand as Barkley wagged his tail and gave an excited *WOOF*.

"It's OK, he's her pet – like Kai," Emily explained.

"Yeah, dogs are like land dolphins," Layla said with a giggle. "They're really playful, loyal and fun. He won't hurt you, promise."

Marina looked at Barkley and tentatively put out her hand to touch his brown fur.

"His scales are so soft!" she said. Barkley rolled on his back for a tummy

tickle and
Marina giggled.
"I see what you
mean. He *is* like
Kai!"

Then her
laughter faded,
and Emily
knew she was
thinking about
her pet and her family back in Atlantis.
"You'll see Kai again," she said firmly,
sounding much more confident than she
felt. "I know you will. First we'll save the
whales, then we'll get you home and save
the wedding!"

"I got some zinc oxide from the surgery," Layla's doctor mum called as she hurried across the sand.

"Oh good," Grace's grandad said.

"What's that for?" Emily asked him.

"The whale expert said to put it around his eyes and blowhole so they don't burn in the sun," Grandad explained.

Layla's mum squeezed some ointment out of the tube and carefully spread some around Piper's eye. Piper squealed and thrashed his tail, making Barkley yelp in fright.

"There, there, it's OK," Layla said, patting Piper's side as her mum put ointment on his other eye.

"Let's get these on him!" Emily's mum said, panting as she arrived back on the beach with her arms full of tablecloths.

Marina and the girls went over to help her, soaking the tablecloths in the sea and then draping the wet fabric over Piper's body. As they covered his tail with a dripping tablecloth, Piper called out and there was an answering call from Cadence in the water. Emily turned to look at the pod anxiously.

"He's so upset!" Marina cried in frustration. "I wish I could talk to him."

"Maybe we can calm him down another way . . ." Emily suggested. Talking about Kai had given her an idea. When they'd rescued Marina's pet dolphin from a fishing net, they'd sung to him. Whales loved music even more than dolphins did, so maybe it would work?

"Let's sing him our song," she said. Trying not to think about the crowd of people all around, Emily focused on Kai. She stroked his side and started to sing.

"The oceans are big and beautiful . . ."

Layla and Grace joined in, the wind sweeping their voices out to the whales in the bay.

"The seas are wide and strong,
But we have to keep them clean . . ."

Marina didn't know the words, but she harmonised with her beautiful voice,

lifting their little song into a stirring
anthem that gave Emily goosepimples.
Next to them, Piper was calm, listening
to the song.

"So join us in our mission,
Save our oceans . . . please."

Even though lots of people in the crowd
had their phones out, taking videos of
the girls singing to the beached whale,
Emily didn't feel self-conscious. She
really believed in what she was singing.

As the last note drifted across the
beach and over the water, lots of people
clapped. But Emily didn't feel happy
at all. Even if they'd managed to calm
Piper, they'd never convince the whales
to leave the harbour without him – and
the tide was going out. If they didn't do
something soon, they wouldn't have one
beached whale, they'd have a whole pod!

Grace's grandad's phone rang and he answered it. His face looked worried. "Well, when *can* they get here?" he said into the phone, looking at the tide in dismay.

"Are the whale rescue team coming soon?" Grace asked him.

"They're struggling to locate the equipment they'll need to move him." Grace's grandad rubbed his neck. "I'm worried about the tide."

Grace glanced at the others and they all nodded. "We can't wait any longer," she said. "We'll just have to find a way to rescue him ourselves!"

Chapter Seven

Grace turned to her grandfather, who was still looking anxiously at the sea as it ebbed away.

"Can't we all push him?" she asked.

Grandad shook his head. "A newborn whale weighs one and a half tonnes. I don't think we could do it even if we had the whole town helping."

Emily glanced at Marina. She couldn't

let her friend have turned human for nothing. "What about your boat?" she asked him.

"*The Salty Seahorse* isn't strong enough either, not without specialist equipment. But maybe more than one boat would do it . . ." Suddenly full of energy, Grandad turned to his sea shanty group. "Luckily, we've got a whole choir of fishermen right here! Right men, we need boats, and lots of 'em. Get to your ships and let's save this whale!"

The sea shanty choir all roared their agreement. "*The Jaunty Jellyfish* will help!" one man said.

"So will *The Dancing Dolphin*,"

another fisherman declared.

"Everyone else," Grandad yelled to the crowd. "You dig a trench in the sand behind the whale, to make him easier to move. We need to make a path down to the sea."

Everyone started talking at once in a buzz of activity. Someone unlocked the boat shed and started handing out kayak paddles and anything that could be used to dig.

"This might come in handy too," said Grace, taking a megaphone from the shed.

The girls each took a paddle and knelt behind one of Piper's fins, digging into

the sand. Other people went back and forth to the sea, pouring water on to the tablecloths that covered Piper, keeping him wet.

Emily dug into the heavy, wet sand. Every time the sea came in it pooled around her knees and she got wet, but she kept digging. She felt so frustrated. Usually as Sea Keepers they could find a solution, but moving such a heavy whale seemed impossible. Tears prickled her eyes as she thought about what would happen if they didn't succeed.

Mum came over and put her arm around her. "We're going to do everything we can to save him," she said.

Emily snuggled into her mum's hug and looked at all the volunteers who had come to help the whale – digging in the sand, fetching water, and racing to get their boats ready for a rescue attempt. Effluvia thought humans were bad, but she was wrong. Most of them were good.

"I'm going to get some food from the

café to keep everyone going. Want to come?" Mum said.

Emily shook her head. "I'll stay with Grace, Layla and Marina," she said. "But thanks, Mum." She felt a bit better.

They kept digging, and soon there was a wide trench around Piper.

"I think that'll do," one of the adults called out. As the girls stood up, Emily's mum and dad arrived with snacks and drinks for everyone.

"Phew!" Grace said, wiping her sandy hand over her sweaty forehead.

Emily was ready for a cool drink – digging in the sand was hard work.

"Ooh, I'm starving!" Layla said.

They ran over to the refreshments
Emily's parents had laid out.

"What's that?" Marina whispered,
pointing at a chocolate muffin.

Layla giggled.

"Let's take a few things for you to try,"

Emily suggested. She grabbed a few bits and they sat down for a picnic.

"Human food is weird!" Marina crinkled her nose as she poked the muffin suspiciously.

"Try it, it's delicious!" Emily urged her.

"Um no, I'm OK," Marina said.

"We tried seaweed curry," Grace reminded her.

"And frostberry ice cream!" Layla added.

"Don't forget the plankton sandwiches," said Emily.

"OK . . ." Marina said hesitantly. She broke off a piece of the muffin and put it in her mouth.

"What do you think?" Emily asked.

Marina pulled a face. "Is it meant to taste like that?" she asked.

Emily took a bite of the muffin and grinned as the sweet chocolate chunks dissolved on her tongue. "Mmm, yes, it's delicious!"

"Here, try this," Grace gave her a can of fizzy lemonade.

"Bleurgh! That's even worse!" Marina coughed and spluttered as the bubbly

drink frothed out of the can.

Layla laughed and opened a big bag of crisps.

"Hey, I recognise that." Marina pointed at the packet. "I've seen those floating in the sea. I didn't know they had food inside them."

"They're called crisps – they're fried potato," Layla explained. "These are salt and vinegar flavoured. Try one!"

Marina tentatively tasted one. "Mmm, that's actually good!"

"I guess it's salty like the sea," Grace thought out loud.

"Well, now I know I like one sort of human food." Marina looked at the sea

sadly. "At least I won't starve."

"Oh, you'll never starve with us around!" Dad interrupted as he came over. "Hello, I don't think we've met."

He held out his hand to Marina, who just stared at it in confusion.

Emily distracted her father with a hug. "Dad, this is Marina," she said.

"How do you girls know each other?" Dad asked.

"We met on the beach," Emily told him. That was true at least. "Marina cares about protecting the sea, just like we do."

Marina nodded, her pinky purple hair bobbing around her face.

"So do you live here in Sandcombe?" asked Dad.

Luckily, a shout from the beach meant that Marina didn't have to answer – and Emily's dad couldn't ask any more awkward questions.

"Everyone! Gather round!" Grace's grandad bellowed.

Emily and her friends went over to him.

A camera crew had arrived from the local news station and was filming the rescue attempt. "You're joining us live from Sandcombe harbour . . ." a reporter said, speaking into a microphone.

Grace's grandad had already tied ropes carefully around Piper's tail. "We're

going to try and pull him out to sea," he told everyone. "We'll take it slow and steady. Those of you on the shore, make sure he doesn't get distressed. If we need to stop, raise your arm and we'll all stop."

He handed the ends of two ropes to fishermen who splashed back through

the shallow water to where *The Dancing Dolphin* and *The Jaunty Jellyfish* were waiting. He handed Grace the megaphone from the boat shed and the end of a rope. "Your job is to get everyone to pull at the same time. Think you can do it?"

Grace nodded.

Taking the end of yet another rope, he waded back to *The Salty Seahorse*.

"Come with me!" Grace yelled to her friends. She waded out to the shallow water, where her dinghy was tied up to a buoy.

"Mum, can I go out in Grace's dinghy?" Emily asked.

"Of course, but wear a lifejacket," Mum called. "We don't want to have to rescue you too! How about you?" she turned to Marina. "Can you swim?"

Marina smiled. "Yeah, I'm pretty good at swimming."

"Come on!" Grace called, and they splashed through the shallow water and climbed onboard the boat.

"I've always wanted to go on a boat!" Marina said excitedly, as Emily helped her into the dinghy.

Grace handed Layla the megaphone. "I've got to steer, so Layla, you give the orders."

Layla's eyes gleamed as she picked up

megaphone. "When I say GO, everyone pull!" she called. "Three, two, one . . . GO!"

Grace started the motor and the dinghy moved out to sea, with Marina

and Emily holding firmly on to the rope
and Layla shouting encouragement
over the megaphone. Piper was tugged
down the beach and Emily felt a surge of
excitement – but then he stopped.

"And again!" Layla bellowed. "PULL!"

But it wasn't enough. Soon Grace's engine was on full throttle, but even with all four boats pulling, they couldn't move Piper into the water.

As Emily pulled, she noticed a dark shadow in the sea next to her. There was a spurt of water as a whale came to the surface to breathe, then sank back down again.

"It would be so easy if they could help us!" Layla said, sighing.

Emily looked at the whale and had an idea. "Maybe they can!"

Chapter Eight

"Quick, get their attention," Emily said, leaning over the side of the dinghy. The girls all splashed the water until the whale's great barnacle-covered head broke the surface of the waves. Viola's small eyes blinked up at them curiously.

"We can't talk to her, but maybe we can make her understand . . ." Emily told the others.

"Hi, Viola," Marina said, stroking the whale's head.

"We need you to PULL," Emily said, grabbing the rope and miming pulling it as hard as she could. "Take it and swim, far out to sea," she said, pointing out of the harbour. Then she dropped the rope into the water.

Viola blinked slowly, and then huffed out a fountain of water which pattered down on them like rain.

"Argh!" Layla cried. "Not again!"

"Does that mean yes?" Grace wondered.

"I hope so!" Emily crossed her fingers.

For a second nothing happened, and Emily's shoulders dropped. She'd been so

sure that Viola had understood . . .

But then the rope started snaking away into the water, faster and faster as the huge whale took it in her mouth and swam out to sea, pulling with a strength greater than ten ships. And on the shore, Piper started to move!

The baby calf slid down the sandy beach. There were shouts of delight from the other boats and celebrations on the shore as he was pulled back into the water. They'd done it!

As the girls watched from the dinghy, volunteers splashed into the water to untie the ropes from Piper's tail. Piper was singing with happiness now, a joyful sound that was echoed by the rest of the pod. As the last rope fell away from his tail, he swam eagerly towards his family.

Grace, Emily, Layla and Marina hugged each other, making the little boat rock from side to side so much they almost fell in.

The people on the beach cheered loudly, kicking up the water and splashing about in celebration.

"I bet you're feeling very pleased with yourselves," came a voice from the side of the dinghy. Effluvia was there in the water next to them, Gulper wrapped around her shoulders and the harp in her arms. "Why don't you go and join them now that Princess Marina has finally become one of the two-legs she so admires!"

Marina gasped. "YOU got me banished!" she said.

"Of course I did!" Effluvia gloated. "I saw you from the water and sent word to

Atlantis. It worked even better than I'd planned. You'll be banished for life – and so will the Sea Keepers!"

"Marina's family will be proud that they have such a brave daughter!" Layla said. "And if they aren't, they don't deserve her!"

Effluvia scoffed. "Ugh, you're so sickening. Even you have to admit I've won this time. Marina is banished, I've still got the harp, and without it no mermaid will ever be able to get married again!" Effluvia laughed as she dived underwater.

"I hate to say it, but I think she's right," Grace said sadly.

Emily nodded. "We can't fight Effluvia from land."

"How are we going to stop her without

a Golden Pearl's magic?" Layla said.

"Stop that!" Marina stood up in the dinghy, pointing the oar at them like a fearsome pirate captain. "It's not the Golden Pearl's magic that makes you brilliant Sea Keepers! It's YOU! You never give up trying to protect sea creatures and the oceans! Now stop. Moaning. And. Start. Thinking!" Marina jabbed the oar at each word, but the effect was ruined when she wobbled and fell over, landing in a heap at the bottom of the boat.

"Stupid human legs!" she grumbled.

Emily, Layla and Grace rushed to help her up. "You're completely right," Emily

told her. "We can't give up."

"Aye, aye, Captain!" Layla added.

"I've got it!" Grace said, holding up a fishing rod. "Maybe instead of thinking like mermaids, we need to think like humans!"

"Yes!" Marina cheered, squeezing all three girls tight. "I knew you'd think of something."

Emily looked at where Grace was fiddling with the fishing rod. "You're going to catch Gulper?" she asked.

"No," Grace replied.

"You're going to catch EFFLUVIA?" Layla gasped, her mouth open wide.

"No!" Grace said, laughing.

"What else is there?" Emily peered down into the water. Through the lapping waves she could just make out the midnight blue of Effluvia's hair, the eel's long, snake-like body, and the shimmering gold of the magic harp. "Oh!" she suddenly realised. "You're going to hook the harp!"

"I'm going to try!" Grace said, flicking back the rod and letting the line sink down into the sea.

The water wasn't that deep, but it wasn't as clear as the ocean in some of the places they'd visited. Emily peered down, willing the hook to connect with the gold harp.

"I think I've got something . . ." Grace
said. She quickly started to turn the
handle to reel the line in. Emily kept her
eyes on the flash of gold in the water . . .

"It's the harp!" Layla said.

"You've got it!" Marina agreed.

"Keep going!" Emily encouraged her.

The golden harp was moving through the water towards them as Grace reeled it in as fast as she could. It was almost at the surface, and Emily, Layla and Marina held out their hands to grab it – but another hand emerged from the water and grabbed it instead.

"Not so fast!" Effluvia snarled.

She yanked the harp and the line started to unreel. Grace was pulled to the edge of the dinghy, but she didn't let go of the rod.

Emily grabbed Grace's middle and

Layla grabbed Emily's. Together, all three girls pulled – and the harp made it to the surface, its golden strings glinting in the sunshine.

But before they could grab it, the line snapped – and the harp plunged back underwater!

Chapter Nine

Layla, Emily and Grace were flung
backwards on to the floor of the dinghy
as the fishing line broke and the harp
plopped back into the sea. Gulper snaked
towards it as it sank, his huge mouth
open wide.

"Noooo!" Marina yelled. She ran to the
edge of the boat . . . and leapt overboard!
A second later she surfaced, and hauled

the harp up into the dinghy.

"Good work, Marina," Layla cried.

"Help!" Marina spluttered, clinging on to the side of the boat. "How do you swim with legs? They won't do what I want!" She looked at her legs crossly.

The girls laughed and pulled her into the boat.

"You'll have plenty of time to learn, two-legs," Effluvia jeered. "After all, you'll never be allowed back to the mermaid world after this."

"The harp!" Emily remembered. "Can you use its power to get your tail back?"

Marina shook her head. "The magic is for Meredith and Zaire to get married,

so I'm going to get it back to them, no matter what."

"You useless worm!" Effluvia yelled at Gulper as he surfaced, his mouth still open wide.

"STOP BEING SO MEAN!" Layla shouted into the megaphone. But her words were drowned out by an ear-splitting crackle of static.

Everyone – including Effluvia – winced at the

sound and covered their ears.

"Oops – sorry," Layla said.

"Actually, I think it helped – look at Gulper's eyes!" Marina said. Sure enough, the eel's eyes weren't yellow any more. The loud shriek of static had broken Effluvia's spell!

Gulper grinned at the girls, then slithered underwater.

"Pah, I don't need you anyway," Effluvia spat as he swam away. "Or the harp. There's something else that can make beautiful music around here – me!"

She looked in the water around her. "Fang!" she commanded. The anglerfish poked his head out of the water and his

mouth opened and shut. Effluvia laughed and looked at the girls in the dinghy triumphantly.

Marina, Grace, Layla and Emily glanced at each other.

"Um, if he's talking to us, we can't understand him," Grace told her.

"Oh, right," Effluvia said. "Well, he said we're going to stop those whales from getting away – and there's nothing you can do about it!"

Effluvia disappeared underwater, with Fang trailing behind her. The wicked siren surfaced in the middle of the harbour and started to sing. The whales had been heading out to sea, but when

they heard the
song they turned
back and circled
around her in a
beautiful ballet
– but one that
would be deadly if
Effluvia got
her way!

"Quick, we
have to stop
her!" Grace
said, starting the
engine. Emily
and Layla picked
up the oars and

148

they set off after Effluvia, but the circling whales had made the waves choppy.

"This isn't working!" Emily said, as another big wave rocked the boat. "The waves are as rough as they are in a storm."

"Wait – didn't the Mystic Clam say something about a storm?" Layla said suddenly.

"He did!" Grace exclaimed. "He said 'when music and friendship work together, any storm you can weather'."

"Maybe he was giving us a clue," said Layla. "We can fight music with music!"

"It's worth a try," said Grace.

Emily groaned. "You're going to make

me sing again, aren't you?"

Layla grinned and linked her arm with Emily's. "If we can sing louder than Effluvia then they might follow us instead," she said, picking up the megaphone again. It crackled and squeaked, but this time Layla's voice came out clear and strong as she started to sing their Sea Keeper song. The others gathered round and Layla held the megaphone out in front of them like a microphone.

"The oceans are big and beautiful . . ." They sang their hearts out.

Surrounded by the whales, Effluvia was still singing too. But there were four of

them, and only one of her – and they had the megaphone. Singing louder and louder, the Sea Keepers were drowning her out!

Loudest of all was Marina's beautiful voice. Emily grinned as she heard it. If Marina couldn't go back to being a mermaid, she could always become a pop star!

The whales stopped circling Effluvia and the water calmed. They were listening!

Emily shut her eyes and raised her voice, singing out to the waves and the listening whales. Suddenly, she heard a spout of water and Layla squealed with delight. Emily opened her eyes to see a whale in front of her.

Still singing, Grace sat down by the rudder. Marina picked up an oar and Emily grabbed the other one, while Layla kept hold of the megaphone. Grace manoeuvred the boat towards the open water – and the whales began to follow.

With an angry cry, Effluvia dived underwater. Emily watched worriedly – what was the evil siren up to?

"Are the whales still following us?" she asked, peering over at the water. She couldn't see them any more, as they'd dived down deep.

"Effluvia must be calling them from

152

underwater!" Marina said. "We're just not loud enough."

But then another noise drifted across the water.

"And barnacles on her bum! Oh! Barnacles on her bum!"

The voices were coming from *The Salty Seahorse*, *The Jaunty Jellyfish* and *The Dancing Dolphin*! The fishing boats pulled alongside the dinghy and the fisherman choir bellowed their sea shanty. Layla's grandad waved his arms as he conducted the singers.

The girls joined in the sea shanty – and after a moment the whales reappeared at the water's surface!

The dinghy led the fishing boats out
of the bay and the whales followed,
leaping out of the water in delight as
they followed the joyful music out to sea.
As soon as the whales passed the harbour
walls, the fishermen let out a cheer.

Grace pulled the dinghy alongside her grandad's boat. Grandad leaned over the side, watching the whales swim into deeper water.

"I've never seen anything like it," he said. "That was almost . . . magical."

Emily grinned. He had no idea!

"What are they chasing?" Grandad said as he looked through some binoculars.

"Can I see?" Emily asked. Grandad passed the binoculars down to her and Emily peered through them. In the distance she could see the splash of a whale's tail, and something else – a flash of midnight-blue hair.

"Oh, I think that's just a buoy," Emily told him as she handed them back, trying to hide her grin. "The whales have chased Effluvia away!" she whispered to the others. "We've done it!"

"Well, that was a bit of excitement!" Grandad said. "Everyone back to shore

now. I'll treat you to a hot chocolate at the café."

"See you there!" Grace said, as the boats turned around and headed back to the harbour.

"That was brilliant!" Layla said.

"You just love that megaphone!" Grace teased.

Emily laughed. But then she noticed one of her friends didn't look happy. Marina wasn't laughing. She was peering over the side of the dinghy, trailing her hand in the water. The water rippled as her tears dripped in it.

Emily nudged her friends, and they went to comfort Marina. They'd saved

the whales – now they had to find a way
to make her a mermaid again!

But before they could say anything,
the water rippled again and a long, silver
nose appeared.

"Kai!" Marina gasped in surprise,
almost falling into the water as she
reached out to hug her pet dolphin.

Kai clicked in delight.

"Oh Kai!" she sobbed. "You found me! Please take the harp back to the palace and tell my family I'm sorry. I only broke the rules to help the whales. I'm going to miss you all so much!"

Kai clicked and Marina wept even louder. "I can't understand you!" she cried.

Kai nuzzled her with his nose. Marina kissed his sleek head. "Well, I understood that," she said through her tears. "If you can understand me, tell Mum and Dad I love them. Even Neptune too. And I love you, Kai. Come back and visit me sometimes, OK?"

Marina put the harp into the water next to the dolphin.

"Why can't you use its magic?" Layla suggested. "I know getting married is important, but so is you being a mermaid!"

Marina shook her head. "It wouldn't be right. The harp's magic is very strong, but if I use it for myself there might not be enough magic left for Meredith's wedding. Please take it back to the palace, Kai." She pointed out to sea. Then she sadly hugged her pet dolphin goodbye.

Suddenly the harp played a beautiful, ethereal sound, and the golden strings turned into a shimmering rainbow which beamed out and surrounded Marina, Kai and the girls.

"What's happening?" Grace yelled.

"I don't know," Marina called back,
"but I think it's mermaid magic!"

Chapter Ten

The magic surrounded Emily, Grace, Layla and Marina in a whirl of multicoloured bubbles. They held hands and laughed as the bubbles spun around them, then suddenly – *POP!* – the bubbles burst and they were back in Atlantis, in the palace courtyard.

"You're a mermaid again!" Layla flung her arms around Marina, and Emily and

Grace joined in too, giving the mermaid princess an enormous hug.

"I'm so happy!" Marina cried, swishing her fins and stroking the lilac-coloured scales of her mermaid tail. "But how did this happen?"

"A-hem," a cough sounded. They turned to see the Mystic Clam, underneath a beautiful coral archway decorated with anemone garlands.

"What are you doing here?" Layla asked him.

The Mystic Clam chuckled. "I'm getting ready to perform a wedding, of course!"

There was a ripple of laughter from behind them and they turned to see a crowd of mermaids watching them from rows of rock seats. A long aisle between the seats led to the archway.

"Everything's set up for the wedding!" Marina whispered.

All the guests were looking at them curiously. Emily noticed lots of mermaids they'd met before on their adventures. There was Anji, the Arctic merfolk's leader, and Calypso, who taught at the Sea Turtle School in the Caribbean. Everyone's tails were gleaming and they wore amazing hats. One mermaid had a starfish perched jauntily on her head, and another wore a whole group of mussels like a beret.

But only the royal mermaids wore crowns. Queen Adrianna, King Caspian and Prince Neptune were swimming towards them now, wearing special crowns made of bright pink coral.

"We brought the magic harp back," Grace said.

"We didn't take it, it was Effluvia!" Layla explained.

To Emily's surprise, Queen Adrianna came over to Marina and gave her an even bigger hug than the girls had.

"I am so proud of you, my brave daughter," she whispered, kissing Marina's head.

"I don't understand," Marina sniffled. "I thought I was going to be banished forever because I turned into a human."

"She was just trying to save the whales," Layla said.

"She wouldn't even use the harp's magic to help herself," Emily added.

"I know." Queen Adrianna nodded.

"That's why you were allowed to come back here," King Caspian said as he hugged Marina.

"The Spirits of the Sea brought you back," Adrianna explained, looking at the harp in wonder. "They are the source of all water magic, and they have made you a mermaid again!"

"Marina!" Meredith cried, swimming out from the palace.

"What are you doing here! The bride should not be seen. Go back inside," Delphine fussed as she swam after her, but Meredith ignored her mum.

She swam over to Marina with her seaweed veil streaming behind her. "I've been so worried about you!"

"We brought you the harp," Marina told her cousin.

"A wedding is nowhere near as important as you are!" Meredith said. "I'm so glad you're back." She turned to the girls. "I owe you a big apology, Sea Keepers. I'm sorry I believed that you took it."

"You're not the only one who owes them an apology," the queen said, pushing Prince Neptune forward.

Neptune looked at the Sea Keepers sulkily. "They took my racing carriage."

"If you don't apologise, I shall give Marina your racing carriage," King Caspian boomed.

"Sorry, Sea Keepers," Neptune muttered.

"It's OK," Emily said kindly. "The most important thing is Marina is home."

"And the whales are safe," added Grace.

"And we beat Effluvia!" Layla said.

"Oh my goodness, look at the tide!" Delphine said. "We have to finish getting ready for the wedding before Zaire arrives!"

"Wait!" Meredith said. "Would you be my bridesmaids, Sea Keepers? After all, I

wouldn't be having a wedding if it wasn't for you."

The girls grinned. "Yes please!" they all said together.

Emily smiled – she'd never been a bridesmaid before, especially not a mermaid bridesmaid!

Grace, Layla and Emily followed the wedding party inside.

"Hang on, let me check something." Marina sang a high note of mermaid magic. Suddenly they were all wearing special bridesmaid outfits and carrying colourful anemone bouquets! Emily had a bright pink top and a starfish tiara. Layla had a purple top and an anemone crown,

and Grace had a shimmering silver top
and a band of seashells over her blonde
hair, which had been plaited and pinned
to match Marina's.

"My magic works again!" Marina said happily.

Delphine fussed about with last-minute preparations, while Marina and the girls helped Meredith arrange her long seaweed veil.

"You look beautiful," Emily told her.

"So do you," Meredith said, grinning at them.

"I can't believe this is my first time being a bridesmaid and I can't tell anyone about it!" Emily said to her friends.

"You can talk about it with us!" Grace told her.

"We'll remember it even when we're

little old ladies," Layla added as the three friends looped arms.

"Zaire's here!" Delphine said.

The girls swam to the window and looked out. A carriage pulled by a huge stingray was arriving at the palace.

"Ready?" Marina asked her cousin.

Meredith nodded.

They made their way back to the courtyard, and a band of trumpetfish began to play. The guests all turned to look, but Meredith only had eyes for the merman waiting for her at the end of the aisle.

She swam forward, perfectly in time with the music, her long veil floating

behind her. Marina and the Sea Keepers swam after her, holding their bouquets.

When they reached the archway, the music stopped. Zaire took Meredith's hand in front of the Mystic Clam.

"Mermaids and mermen," the Mystic Clam intoned. "It is my great pleasure to welcome you here to the wedding of our dear friends, Meredith and Zaire."

He paused, and for a second Emily worried that he'd fallen asleep.

"Whale song blessing!" Marina whispered.

"Ah, yes," the old clam said. "We will begin with the whale song blessing."

Marina swam over to where Viola

176

and the other whales were waiting. She picked up the harp and started to sing.

As Marina's voice blended with the whale song, the harp's strings turned into a rainbow again. The rainbow arced through the water and surrounded the happy couple in coloured light.

Kai swam over, balancing two rings on his nose. Still in the rainbow light, Meredith and Zaire took them, and turned to look at each other.

"Meredith and Zaire, do you promise to love each other in good tides and bad tides, in the shallows and the deep, in stormy seas and calm seas?" the Mystic Clam asked them.

"We do," Meredith and Zaire said together.

"Well then, by the power of the Spirits of the Sea, I now pronounce you married," he explained.

As Meredith and Zaire kissed, the merfolk started applauding. The whales sang out again, and the rainbow light spread out from Meredith and Zaire and bathed the whole congregation in its glow.

Emily hugged Grace and Marina hugged Layla.

Delphine clapped her hands and a team of turtles came out of the palace balancing platters of food on their shells.

There was an enormous wedding cake painted with starfish, huge plates of plankton sandwiches, bowls of kelp salad and a huge heap of frostberry ice cream.

"Real food!" Marina yelled. Laughing and chatting, everyone swam over to the refreshments and started helping themselves.

"Humans have these things called salt and vinegar crisps," Emily heard Marina telling the other guests as she filled her plate.

After they'd eaten, the rock seats were cleared away and the courtyard became a dance floor. There was an octopus DJ and a sea urchin disco ball! The girls

danced until their fins ached. Even the Mystic Clam was opening and shutting his shell to the beat.

"I need to take a break," panted Emily.

"Just one more dance!" Layla begged. She grabbed her friends and they spun round happily.

When the song finished they made their way over to where Marina was chatting to the happy couple.

"Sea Keepers, meet my husband, Zaire," Meredith introduced them to the groom.

"Congratulations!" Layla said.

Zaire gave a low bow. "It's an honour to meet you," he said. "I have you to thank for retrieving the magic harp."

181

"You're welcome," Emily said.

"Thanks for letting us share your special day," said Grace.

"Meredith and Zaire are about to leave on their honeymoon," Marina told them. The newlyweds climbed into Zaire's stingray carriage and left the party, waving as they went.

"We should probably go, too," Emily told Marina.

"I loved seeing Sandcombe, but I'm

182

so glad I'm not going with you!" Marina said. "I'll call you again as soon as the Mystic Clam remembers where another pearl is."

"Or if there's another brilliant mermaid party for us to go to!" Layla suggested.

"Maybe next time Effluvia won't try to spoil it," said Grace.

"I think Effluvia will always try to cause trouble," Marina said. "But luckily we have you Sea Keepers to stop her!" She hugged the girls, and sang the magic words to send them home:

**"Send the Sea Keepers back to land
Until we need them to lend a hand."**

With a whoosh, the girls were back

in the dinghy, heading back to shore.
Because of the magic, no one had even
noticed they'd gone.

"That was amazing!" Layla exclaimed.
"Now, didn't your grandad say something
about a hot chocolate, Grace?"

The harbour was still busy with people
who'd helped with the whale rescue.

Emily's mum and dad raced over as the
girls pulled the dinghy on to the sand.
Barkley ran up to them too, barking and
wagging his tail.

"Emily, the reporter wants to interview
you girls!" Mum said.

"Try and mention the café and our
delicious coffee!" Dad whispered.

The camera crew came over. "Here we are with the three girls that found the whale!" the reporter said. She frowned. "Wasn't there another girl, with pink and purple hair?"

"She had to go home," Layla said, grinning.

"What did you think when you saw the whale?" the reporter asked Grace.

"We knew we had to help it," she replied.

The reporter nodded, then she stuck the microphone in front of Emily's face. "Do you have a message for our viewers?"

Emily panicked for a moment, wondering what she should say. Then the

words of their song sprang into her mind and she leaned into the microphone. "We have to protect our seas. We need to stop using plastic and dumping it in the sea, and we have to clean up and put right what we've got wrong. Everyone – please join us in our mission!"

"Well said!" The reporter nodded again. "Well, this is me, signing off from Sandcombe Bay, the scene of a dramatic whale rescue with a very happy ending. I bet this is the biggest adventure you girls have ever had!"

"Oh, you have no idea!" Emily said with a grin. Then she linked arms with her best friends and followed the crowd back up the hill to the café for a well-earned hot chocolate!

The End

Join Emily, Grace and Layla
for another adventure in …

Seal Pup Party

Grace looked around the lounge
and grinned in glee. It was all so
Christmassy! The Christmas tree in the
corner was filled with decorations and
twinkly lights and there was holly draped
over the fireplace. Grandad was in his
usual armchair, looking at his phone,
and her dog Barkley was laid out in front
of the cosy fire, snoring happily. Just
then he sat up and pricked an ear, and
a second later the doorbell rang and a

carol started from outside. *"Silent Night, Holy Night . . . "*

"Ooh, carol singers!" Grace's little brother Henry dropped his game and ran to the door.

"That's not carol singers," Grace said, laughing as she barged ahead of him to open it.

Her best friends Emily and Layla were huddled on the doorstep. Behind them, the sea was dark and choppy, the waves splashing up onto the beach.

"Sleep in heavenly peace!" Layla sang dramatically, flinging out her arms as Emily giggled.

"Come in, quick, it's freezing out

there!" Mum called.

Grace ushered her friends into the toasty warm cottage and helped them hang up their coats and hats on the rack.

"Right, bakers, I've left everything out for you in the kitchen, try not to make too much of a mess," Grace's mum said as she came to greet them. It was Christmas Eve, and Emily and Layla had come round to bake mince pies for Santa.

They kitchen was soon full of laughter and more carol singing as the girls rolled out the pastry and filled it with the delicious mincemeat. Grace was carefully putting the mince pies in the oven when Henry gave a yelp from the lounge.

Grace poked her head out to see what was happening. Henry was standing by a pile of Christmas stockings and sucking his finger. "The holly spiked me!" he complained.

The girls went over to the fireplace to help. "Argh!" Layla cried out as she moved the holly.

Read Seal Pup Party
to find out what happens next!

SEA KEEPERS

Dive into a mermaid adventure!

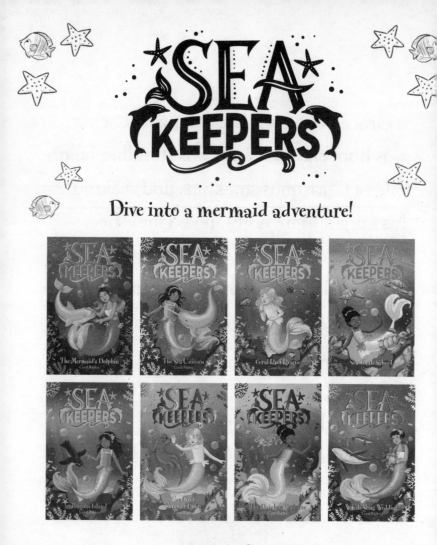

The Mermaid's Dolphin · Coral Ripley
The Sea Unicorn · Coral Ripley
Coral Reef Rescue · Coral Ripley
Sea Turtle School · Coral Ripley
Penguin Island · Coral Ripley
Sea Otter Summer Camp · Coral Ripley
The Rainbow Seahorse · Coral Ripley
Whale Song Wedding · Coral Ripley

Coming Soon

Seal Pup Party · Coral Ripley
The Missing Manatee · Coral Ripley
Starfish Sleepover · Coral Ripley